To Aniba and
Ja

From!

Roses
are
red,
vilots
are
blue,
candy
is sweet
and I Love
you!

Supriya and
Elshan

XOXO

MW01104876

OM SHRI RAM!　　　　OM SHRI RAM!
OM SHANTHI SHANTHI SHANTHI HI!

Ramayana

A Children's Epic

An Epic Originally Written by Sage
Valmiki

By

Girish Rathnam Swaminath

authorHOUSE™

1663 LIBERTY DRIVE, SUITE 200
BLOOMINGTON, INDIANA 47403
(800) 839-8640
WWW.AUTHORHOUSE.COM

First published by AuthorHouse 11/30/04

ISBN: 1-4184-0382-2 (e)
ISBN: 1-4184-0381-4 (sc)

Library of Congress Control Number: 2004096541

Printed in the United States of America
Bloomington, Indiana

This book is printed on acid-free paper.

The Ramayana is an epic about the adventures of Rama, Seetha, and Lakshmana.

These princes are happy until one of their mothers Kaikeyi makes them stay in the forest because of her jealousy. During their journey, Rama kills many people and Seetha gets kidnapped by a rakshasa or demon. Rama fights with the rakshasa.

This is a moral story of love, happiness, sorrow, warfare, and struggle. Will Rama kill Ravana and take Seetha back to Ayodhya? How will people at Ayodhya react to the struggles of the trio? Read the book to find out.

INTRODUCTION

"Om Shuklam Bharadharam Vishnum

Sashivarnam Chathurbhujam

Prasanna Vadhanam Dhayaayet

Sarvavighno Upashaanthaye."

You may have heard about this mantra. This mantra in Sanskrit is used in poojas. From prehistoric times when people first came to this earth to today, many Hindus recite this mantra. Lord Vishnu is part of the Hindu Trinity which includes Lord Brahma, Lord Vishnu, and Lord Shiva. Lord Vishnu is the god of the gods and is one of the strongest gods in the vaikuntha or heaven. He has four hands: one hand holds a discus, another holds a lotus, while the other two hold a mace and a conch. His vehicle is Garuda, a fast bird that spreads Vedic knowledge to all Hindus. He sleeps on a serpent called Seshnag. Lord Vishnu is the hero of the Ramayana and behind it is an important reason.

One day, when Lord Vishnu's wife Goddess Lakshmi was massaging his legs after a long day, some devotees sang:

"Shaanthaa Kaaram Bujagashayanam Padmanaabham Suresham
Vishwadhaaram Gagana Sadhirsham
Megha Varnam Shubangam
Lakshmi Kaantham Kamalanayanam Yogi Hridhyaana Gamyam
Vande Vishnum Bava Bhaya Haram Sarva Lokaika Naatham."

As the devotees sang, Lord Vishnu woke up. They said, "Oh Lord Vishnu, We adore you, the avatharam of peace, who lies on the Seshnag serpent, thy navel is the source of the lotus, and thy appearance is dark like the clouds. Your body shines with heavenly beauty. Oh Lord! You are the husband of wealth (Goddess Lakshmi) and your eyes are like a lotus. The yogis worship you, the remover of fear. We yogis have come here because of a problem."

"May I know the difficulties you are facing, my devotees?"

"A rakshasa named Ravana is destroying the whole world. None of the devas could kill him. We have come to you for help to resolve this problem."

"I shall fulfill my devotees' wishes. It will happen tomorrow, when I will go to earth as a kshatriya to kill Ravana. He has to die and I swear to do it."

1. THE YAGA

Ayodhya was one of the holiest and most beautiful kingdoms of Bharat (India). A delightful breeze and blazing sun soothed Ayodhya's citizens. Oh! How beautiful it was in the morning. People were waiting in line to bathe in the Ganga River. Children were dancing and running with each other. Those who exercised spent a long time waiting in line to drink coconut water. On the southern bank, there was an enormous grassland which led to a forest. Servants even swam across the Ganga River just to get the mouth-watering apples and oranges to sell them along the riverside. Bazaars and stalls were occupying the riverside. Next to the fruit trees were nice carnations and sunflowers. Ayodhya was known for the flowers' sweet smell. However, on the northern bank of the river, it was very quiet and peaceful. Groups of vaishyas were discussing trade and some were herding and farming in the agricultural part of Ayodhya.

On the northern bank of the river, there was a red palace where the royal family lived. The royal family included King Dasharatha, Queen Kaushalya, Queen Sumitra, and Queen Kaikeyi. They had a problem.

They never had children. Dasharatha was concerned about this and tried many times to have children but nothing worked out.

One day, Dasharatha asked his messenger to call for Sumantha. He was Dasharatha's royal charioteer. Sumantha approached him and asked him, "Please accept my greetings, my king. Why did you call me?"

"I called you to talk about something. I don't have any children and I have tried everything to have children."

"I have an idea. You can perform a yaga to Lord Agni. He might give you a boon and you can use that boon for having children."

"May you live long. You have given me the best idea. We shall immediately arrange for the yaga. We shall have it tomorrow."

The day passed and the yaga was arranged. Dasharatha and his wives sat in front of some fire and kept on pouring ghee into the fire. Sage Vasishta conducted the yaga. They continuously prayed for two hours and suddenly Lord Agni appeared right in front of them. He said, "I am satisfied with your devotion and meditation. The boon you shall have is children. I will give you some payasam which you have to give to your wives. Take the payasam and wait for two days. Then, you will have children." Then, he vanished. Dasharatha fed the payasam to his wives and waited for a while.

2. AYODHYA'S ENLIGHTENMENT

After two months, a messenger notified Dasharatha of four births. Every single queen gave birth to one son, except for Sumitra, who gave birth to two sons. Dasharatha came to know about that. He was very happy that he had four sons. After two weeks, the sages came to name the babies. Kaushalya's son was named Rama (the avatharam of Vishnu), Sumitra's two sons were named Lakshmana and Shatrughna, and Kaikeyi's son was named Bharata.

Rama was a boy who would do anything his parents told him to do no matter if he liked it or not. His best quality was determination. He was a kind-hearted boy and he was never angry. Lakshmana was angry sometimes. However, he always listened to Rama. Rama and Lakshmana could not live without each other. Bharata and Shatrughna also listened to Rama. Bharata and Shatrughna also were loyal to each other.

The four brothers celebrated their Upanayanams and gave alms to their guru, Vasishta. They learned archery. Rama was extremely perfect at archery. His brothers were also good but Rama was superior to all of them. Rama always played games with bows and arrows during his childhood. Lakshmana, Bharata, and Shatrughna were very cautious and were confident.

3. THE DEATH OF TATAKA

One day, Sage Vishwamitra approached King Dasharatha. He said, "Oh Your Highness, please don't mistake me but could I take Rama to kill Tataka, the rakshasi who has been destroying the forest?"

"Don't you know his age? Rama is only fifteen years old. He cannot already start to kill rakshasas. He is so precious to me."

"But my king, Rama is one of the bravest princes I have ever seen. If you want I can also take Lakshmana with me. You don't know his strength my king. When he was five, he never missed the target I set up for him. He was so good that he was my favorite disciple. Please, Your Honor. I wouldn't ask for anything more."

"Well alright. Now I am convinced and confident. I think that you have helped me do a good deed. But will you return quickly? Be careful too!"

Therefore, Sage Vishwamitra took Rama and Lakshmana to the forest. He was showing her the rakshasi Tataka. She was as scary and ferocious as a monster killing all the people on Earth. She was the ugliest woman that Rama ever saw. Rama started to battle Tataka. It was a piece of cake for Rama to fight Tataka. Tataka tried to dodge Rama's arrows. Rama was fighting with his arrows. He struck an arrow right into Tataka's chest. Tataka had blood just like two bottles of ketchup spilled. Lakshmana, Rama, and Sage Vishwamitra were very happy to see the death of Tataka.

4. THE CURSE OF GAUTAMA

Sage Vishwamitra was walking to Ayodhya and on the way, they started a conversation about Sage Gautama's curse.

Years back, Lord Indra wanted to marry Anandhi, Sage Gautama's wife. One day, Sage Gautama went for a yaga but he left his wife behind.

At the vaikuntha, Lord Indra said to his subjects, "I have heard about Anandhi's beauty. I am going to Earth as Sage Gautama to kidnap her and make her my queen. Until then, the prime minister will take care."

Lord Indra reached Earth and told Anandhi to follow him. Before they could escape, Sage Gautama saw her and said, "Oh my god! I never realized that you would do such a thing. I, Sage Gautama, hereby curse you that you shall be turned into a stone and nobody except Rama will make you back as a human!"

Rama, Lakshmana, and Sage Vishwamitra went to Sage Gautama's hut. It was a deserted place with a stone in it. There was barely enough room to walk. The three people were searching for the stone for a few minutes. They found the stone. Rama touched the stone and the stone became a human. The human who was actually Anandhi was crying due to happiness of being released from the curse. She said, "You have saved my life, my son. You should be happy and successful throughout your life." Rama later left the hut.

5. THE SWAYAMVARA

Sage Vishwamitra asked Rama and Lakshmana if they wanted to go to a swayamvara for Princess Seetha in Mithila. Rama and Lakshmana said that they wanted to go to the swayamvara so the three left to Mithila There were many princes and kings who were in the swayamvara. Seetha was coming from her room with a pottu, two earrings, flowers, a saree, bangles, a metti, and a golusu. She was as beautiful as a peacock. All the princes were so shocked about this.

In the court of Mithila, King Janaka said, "I, King Janaka, ruler of Mithila, am going to explain the rules of the swayamvara for my daughter Princess Seetha. This swayamvara is only for kshatriyas or Brahmins. No Vaishyas or Sudras are allowed to compete in this swayamvara. In the center of the court is the Bow of Mahadeva. Whoever can break this shall get married to Seetha. Understood?"

All the princes and kings were arrogant but they could not lift the bow. Rama was the last one to try. He paused for a moment and then successfully lifted the bow. The bow was broken in a second and it made noise like thunder. Seetha was very pleased to see Rama. Seetha agreed to marry Rama by putting a garland over Rama's neck.

Sage Parashurama arrived at Mithila and told Rama that it is disrespectful to Lord Shiva for breaking His bow and Parashurama objected to the marriage. Fortunately, Lakshmana convinced him that the wedding should take place, and Parashurama returned to his Ashram.

Meanwhile, Janaka sent his messenger to Ayodhya to invite Rama's parents. It took the messenger three days to get to Ayodhya. Janaka's messenger told the royal family in Ayodhya and the citizens of Ayodhya that Rama had won Mithila Princess Seetha in a swayamvara. When Dasharatha and his wives heard the news, they were so happy that they almost fell unconscious. Dasharatha told his charioteer Sumantha to arrange for a ride to Mithila happily.

6. THE PROPOSAL

When the royal family reached Mithila, Janaka was very happy. Janaka arranged for a special hall so that he can talk to Dasharatha, Kaikeyi, Sumitra, and Kaushalya. The hall had real flowers placed next to each other on the wall.

Janaka asked them, "Would you like to accept my elder daughter Seetha as your daughter-in-law?" They all said yes in a group. Janaka thought, "I think I should give my other daughters off to marriage right now to Rama's brothers."

Janaka asked Dasharatha, "Would you like to accept my daughter Urmila to Lakshmana, my daughter Madhavi to Bharata, and my daughter Srutakriti to Shatrughna?"

Dasharatha, Kaikeyi, Kaushalya, and Sumitra thought that this was the happiest moment in their life. They happily accepted the proposal and were happy because this was like reconciliation with Mithila.

7. THE WEDDING OF FOUR COUPLES

Arrangements were already made and everyone in Mithila and Ayodhya were happy. The hall was very elegant and beautiful. In the brides' room, Seetha, Madhavi, Urmila, and Srutakriti were looking fabulous. Seetha was wearing an Orissa Silk Saree while Urmila was wearing a Bengal Cotton Saree. Madhavi and Srutakriti were both wearing a Kanchipuram Silk Saree. They were all wearing pottus and bangles which made them glow. They also wore a golusu and a metti. They put on shining earrings. Meanwhile, Rama put on a Jarigai veshti. Lakshmana put on a blue Kasi Pattu veshti. Bharata and Shatrughna were wearing a Mayilkan veshti. The brides and grooms were ready to go to the marriage hall. The brides did the Gowri pooja.

The wedding hall was covered with vilakus and real colored flowers on the wall. Rama, Lakshmana, Bharata, and Shatrughna were wearing their veshtis and they were ready to take a head bath to begin the marriage ceremony. They took their head baths and then they were ready with their malais. Rama and Lakshmana wore a malai with red and white roses. Bharata and Shatrughna wore a malai with pink roses and green flowers. Then the four brides, wearing the same malais as the grooms, came out of their dressing rooms, and went into the hall.

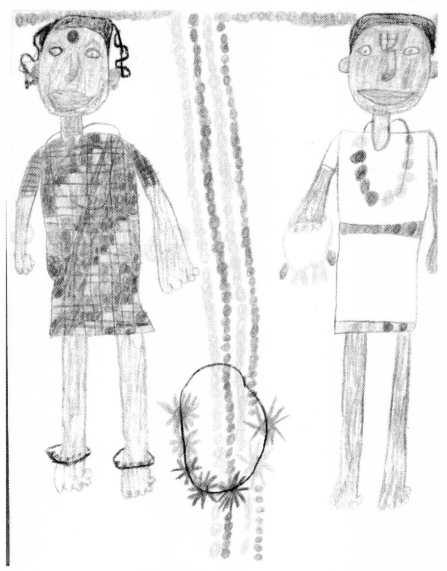

The brides and grooms were in an area covered with orange flowers. Sage Vasishta and Sage Vishwamitra were conducting all four of the weddings.

Sage Vasishta had brought new six-threaded poonals to signify marriage. He made the grooms say the Gayathri Mantra and exchange them.

Sage Vishwamitra told Bharata and Shatrughna to say the Gayathri Mantra and they said it. Then finally , both the sages asked Rama to recite the marriage mantra. Rama tied the wedding chain on Seetha's neck, Lakshmana tied the wedding chain on Urmila's neck, Bharata tied the wedding chain on Madhavi's neck, and Shatrughna tied the wedding chain on Srutakriti's neck. Everyone threw flowers.

There was a large feast. There were bowls of channa batura, gobi paratha, muli paratha, aloo paratha, braki paratha, paneer paratha, spinach paratha, channa paratha, malai kofta, jalebi, mysore paaku, yogurt rice with vepalakatti, chapatti, mixed vegetable curry, sambar, rasam, cootu, rice, dosai, idli, aviyal, chili powder, caseri, dhokla, rasmalai, bhaji, murukku, poori, sev puri, kasta kachori, papdi chaat, and some gulab jamun on the table. There were so many people that all the food was eaten.

Janaka said goodbye to his daughters and they went to Ayodhya with their husbands. Sumantha took the family back to Ayodhya and they went through a very scenic route. It took them three days to get back to Ayodhya. In Ayodhya, some citizens had planned a surprise party. The citizens took the family to the hall. There were people playing the tabla, the violin, singing, and playing the morsing. They played almost all the Ragas with thalas and gamakas in Carnatic and Hindustani music. Some people were dancing.

8. RAMA'S FAILED PATTABISHEKAM

After 5 years, Dasharatha decided that he was getting very old so he wanted to crown Rama as King of Ayodhya. Dasharatha told his minister that he wanted to crown Rama as King of Ayodhya. Soon, the news spread across Ayodhya. All the arrangements were made. Everyone was happy when they heard the news. Rama was also happy that he was going to be the King of Ayodhya. Lakshmana, Bharata, and Shatrughna were also happy for Rama. Kaikeyi, Kaushalya, and Sumitra were also very happy. Bharata and Shatrughna later went to their uncle's house in Kaikeya for a few days.

Manthara, Kaikeyi's companion, however, was the only person in Ayodhya who was very angry to hear the news of Rama's coronation. She wanted Rama to be in exile in the forest and Bharata to be King of Ayodhya. She wanted to go to Kaikeyi's room. When she reached Kaikeyi's room, she was thinking about poisoning Kaikeyi's mind into asking Dasharatha to make Bharata the king of Ayodhya instead of Rama and to send Rama into the jungles out of Ayodhya.

Manthara said, "Hello Kaikeyi," and Kaikeyi said hello to Manthara. Manthara was sneakily talking as if she was happy about Rama's coronation.

Later Manthara said, "Demand for your rights so that you can make your son king."

Kaikeyi replied, "I don't want Bharata to become king. Anyway, our tradition for generations is to make the eldest son king and I also support Rama."

Manthara said, "Your husband Dasharatha has been spoiling Kaushalya and Rama more than you and Bharata."

Kaikeyi said, "Who are you to poison my mind? Who cares about you idiotic lady? I never realized that you were this mean before."

Manthara said, "I am not poisoning your mind. What in the world are you thinking about? You have misunderstood me. Dasharatha is not giving you enough rights."

Kaikeyi was quiet for a moment and after reflecting, she said, "You have a point Manthara. Sorry for all the bad things I have said to you and you are a sweet person. What should I tell Dasharatha?"

Manthara said, "Remember the time in which the Devas fought against the rakshasas? You were a good charioteer to Dasharatha and he was amazed at you so he gave you two boons. He told you that you can choose the two boons anytime and you didn't choose the boons yet. Here is the time in which you can ask the boons. Ask him tomorrow, right before the coronation. Take off all your jewelry and nice costumes. Go to the Hall of Displeasure and lie down in a black dress. He will ask his companion where you are and he will come to you. Talk as if you want Rama to be king. Later, ask him for

these following boons: Ask him to make Bharata king instead of Rama. Ask him also to send Rama to the jungles for fourteen years." Kaikeyi agreed to do that.

9. AYODHYA'S FALL

It was the day of Rama's coronation and it was almost five o'clock in the morning when everybody woke up. Kaikeyi woke up at four o'clock in the morning to take off all her jewelry and to wear black clothes. She went to the Hall of Displeasure before anybody woke up. Everyone was getting ready for the coronation. Ayodhya was very bright. The decorations were very beautiful. Meanwhile, Kaikeyi went to the Hall of Displeasure with a black dress and with no jewelry. She was lying down without any pillows, comforters, or blankets. Rama already took his auspicious bath before the ceremony. Dasharatha was looking for Kaikeyi because she was not present at the hall. He asked his companion where Kaikeyi is and he said that she was at the Hall of Displeasure. Dasharatha was very shocked. Why was she at the Hall of Displeasure?

Dasharatha went to the Hall of Displeasure to find Kaikeyi. Dasharatha asked her, "Why are you in the hall of Displeasure?"

24

Kaikeyi said, "Remember you granted me two boons during the war between the Devas and the Rakshasas? I want you to grant me those boons."

Dasharatha said, "I will grant you any boon you want. Just tell me the boon and I will be happy to give you the boon."

Kaikeyi said, "My first boon is to make Bharata king instead of Rama and my second boon is to send Rama to the jungles for fourteen years."

Dasharatha said sadly, "You sinner, are you trying to ruin the traditions of the clan? Are you trying to ruin my fatherhood and to separate me from my elder son? Are you trying to kill me slowly? It was a big mistake to marry you. What am I going to say to my other wives, Rama and my other sons, and the citizens of Ayodhya? I have to give you the boon because it is against Dharma to refuse to give a boon."

Dasharatha was crying and he fell of his bed in shock. He could not get up. He was mad at Kaikeyi. A messenger saw the whole incident and informed everybody in Ayodhya before the coronation ceremony happened. Everyone was angry with Kaikeyi including Dasharatha, Lakshmana, Kaushalya, Sumitra, Seetha, Madhavi, Urmila, Srutakriti, the citizens of Ayodhya, and Dasharatha's subjects. People

were all saying that Kaikeyi is a mean, rotten woman who wants to ruin Ayodhya's history of happiness. They were all sad because Rama will soon be leaving. Nobody wanted Rama to go to the jungles for fourteen years.

10. RAMA HEARING THE NEWS

Rama went to the Hall of Displeasure to see Dasharatha and Kaikeyi. Rama said, "Did I do anything wrong?"

Kaikeyi replied angrily, "Go ask your father."

Dasharatha said, "No, but this sinner did something wrong. She wanted you to go to the jungles for fourteen years and she wanted Bharata to be king instead of you. I don't want that to happen. I had to give her the boon because it is against Dharma to refuse to give a boon. Please don't go to the forest."

Rama said, "Whatever my parents say, I have to listen to them whether it is good or bad. Please forgive me father but I have to follow your orders because it is against Dharma to disobey my parents."

Everybody wanted to go with Rama. Lakshmana wanted to go with Rama but Rama wanted to go alone. After some influencing, Rama finally wanted to take Lakshmana with him. Everyone else wanted to come but Rama did not want to take anybody. Seetha wanted to go with Rama but Rama again refused. After some influencing by Seetha, Rama wanted to take her with him. Rama refused to take anybody else. Dasharatha wanted his charioteer Sumantha to drive his chariot during his exile period. Rama had no choice but to let everybody come with him.

Dasharatha could not get up having become paralyzed with sorrow. Everyone followed Rama, Lakshmana, Seetha, and Sumantha. They followed them until they slept. Dawn broke when Rama, Lakshmana, Seetha, and Sumantha woke up. It was raining with gray clouds as if the Devas were weeping. Everybody else was sleeping and Rama, Lakshmana, Seetha, and Sumantha decided to leave before anybody wakes up and decides to follow them. They left on their chariot. Meanwhile, one person woke up and said that the four people were gone. Later, everybody woke up and went back to Ayodhya because they did not know where the four people were. Rama, Lakshmana, Seetha, and Sumantha were passing leaves that were very green. They were going over dirty grounds.

11. SUMANTHA BACK AT AYODHYA

Sumantha asked, "We are one foot away from the border between Ayodhya and Kosala. May I stop here?" Rama said yes. He went off the chariot and took some soil from the ground. He put it on the floor again with both of his hands as if he was doing a pooja and he prayed since he is crossing the border from his birthplace. Rama said that Sumantha could return to Ayodhya. Sumantha said goodbye sadly to Rama, Seetha, and Lakshmana because he was to return to Ayodhya with his chariot.

When Sumantha reached Ayodhya, Dasharatha asked him, "Why didn't you stay longer with my son? You could have stayed with Rama. How is my son doing? Is he thinking about me?"

Sumantha said, "I had to follow Rama's orders because he told me to go back to Ayodhya. He is thinking about you. Lakshmana and Seetha are fine and are thinking about you. Lakshmana is angry with Kaikeyi still. I am going to miss Rama."

12. THE EXILE

Meanwhile, the trio (Rama, Lakshmana, and Seetha) crossed the Gomathi River. Before crossing the Gomathi River, the birds formed a musical tune, the water was fresh and it was moving slowly. The sun was shining right on their eyes and there was a mild marine-west-coast climate with moist air. Rama, Lakshmana, and Seetha slowly crossed the river after a farewell from nearby villagers. The river water was very warm. They also crossed the Syandika River where Rama, Lakshmana, and Seetha saw many hunters. They were very friendly and Rama, Lakshmana, and Seetha made many friends who provided them food and shelter. They also questioned the trio why they were in the forest instead of the palace.

Lakshmana replied, "My mother Kaikeyi asked my father Dasharatha for two boons: to push us three into the forest for fourteen years and to make my brother Bharata king instead of my brother Rama." The hunters and villagers were criticizing Kaikeyi for kicking her children and daughter-in-law out of the palace.

Rama said, "Mother Kaikeyi is not mean, she is nice (as Rama never says anything negative about his parents)."

The trio later waved goodbye to the hunters and villagers and they crossed the Sarayu River. Before crossing the Ganga River, gandharvas were singing in praise of Lord Shiva and Lord Vishnu. One gandharva was singing in front of Rama in praise of Lord Vishnu. He did namaskaram to Rama and he said abhivaadaye to him. Rama gave him his blessing. Rama later met Guha, the chieftain of hunters and Guha made a bed for Lakshmana, Rama, and Seetha. The trio made many friends here and they were happy to see them. Guha was gave Rama all the comforts that he asked for including a boat to cross the mighty river Ganga in which women and men were bathing and fetching water. Rama, Lakshmana, and Seetha crossed the Ganga after Guha's farewell.

Rama was thinking about his relatives back in Ayodhya and Kaikeya. He was thinking about the tribulations that his mother Kaikeyi caused and the sorrow of his father Dasharatha and his mothers Sumitra and Kaushalya. He requested Lakshmana to go back to Ayodhya but Lakshmana wanted to stay with his brother Rama and his sister-in-law Seetha. The trio walked towards the Triveni Sangamam to Sage Bharadwaja's Ashram. The maharishi was chanting the Vedas.

Rama said, "Maharishi, I am the son of King Dasharatha of Ayodhya and I am Rama. Here is my brother Lakshmana and my wife Seetha who is the daughter of King Janaka of Mithila. My father has commanded me to live in the forest for a long time. Please accept my respectful greetings. Please suggest us a place where we can be away from people and spend our time meditating."

Sage Bharadwaja said, "Rama, there is a place called Chitrakuta where there are only beautiful lakes and waterfalls and rishis. There are also beautiful fruit trees and caves. I think Chitrakuta is an ideal place for someone like you." Rama and Lakshmana recited their abhivaadaye and did a namaskaram for him. The maharishi recited special mantras since Rama was going on a long journey. Rama was thinking about Sage Bharadwaja's words after he left the ashram.

Rama said to Lakshmana, "I know Seetha admires flowers so if she wants a flower, please give it to her."

They reached Chitrakuta at dawn the next day. A peacock that had blue, green, and red flowers came towards Seetha who really loved it. The birds were whistling and they made music that sounded like a flute. On the way, they saw Sage Valmiki's Ashram. Rama performed a pooja so that he could pray to Lord Narayana and Lord Rudra. Lakshmana worked inside the hermitage. Seetha cooked for Rama and Lakshmana. Their life at Chitrakuta was more peaceful than their life at Ayodhya.

13. THE DEATH OF DASHARATHA

At Ayodhya, everyone was grieving for Rama, Lakshmana, and Seetha. Dasharatha has become paralyzed due to the unbearable separation and he could not get up without assistance. He thought he was going to die. He was very sick. He was sleeping one day and he suddenly remembered something. When he was the prince of Ayodhya, he was practicing to shoot with his bow and arrow by himself. He accidentally attacked a small sixteen-year-old boy who was very skinny. He was starving and he went to fetch water from the Ganga River because his family was dehydrated. Dasharatha was very sad when he accidentally shot the boy. Dasharatha decided to look for the boy's parents and give water to them. He gave water to them and he told them sadly that he accidentally shot their son. The mother died right in front of Dasharatha and the father said, "I hereby curse this boy that when he is separated from his son, he will die." The father immediately died of dehydration too. The curse became true and Dasharatha died due to separation from Rama.

In the morning when all the women in Ayodhya except Kaushalya and Sumitra woke up, they did not realize that Dasharatha had died. His last word was "Rama." The curse had an effect on Dasharatha right now. The women tried to wake him up and they thought he was sleeping. Then they finally felt his body and found out that Dasharatha was dead. They were all very sad. They woke Kaushalya, Sumitra, and Kaikeyi up and told them the terrible truth about the king's death. Everybody cried. People were next to Dasharatha's room. Kaikeyi, the bad sinner, had finally realized that making Bharata king instead of Rama, making Rama live in the jungle for fourteen years, and making Dasharatha cry when he was separated from Rama was a very bad mistake. Kaikeyi, Sumitra, and Kaushalya sadly put on the widows' clothes. Ayodhya was very dark even in the morning. Now the city of happiness had become a city of sorrow.

Kaikeyi paged for her husband's messenger and said, "Please go to Kaikeya and ask Bharata and Shatrughna to come back to Ayodhya immediately."

14. BHARATA AT AYODHYA

Bharata and Shatrughna reached Ayodhya and they were curious to find out why people were not happy. Bharata went to Kaikeyi and saw her wearing no jewelry and she wore widow clothes.

Bharata asked her, "Why don't you have any gold chains or sparkling sarees? Why do the people have their faces down?"

Kaikeyi replied, "I don't know how to say this but your father Dasharatha is dead." Bharata was very shocked and he was crying and he almost fell down unconscious.

Bharata said sadly, "I am going to see Rama and Lakshmana."

Kaikeyi said, "Rama and Lakshmana aren't in Seetha's garden or even in the palace."

Bharata asked, "Where are they then?"

Kaikeyi replied, "I was in a bad mood one day and I wanted to ask your father two boons: to banish Rama out of Ayodhya for fourteen years and to make you the king instead of Rama. Seetha also went with your brothers."

Bharata said, "You insane woman, I am ashamed to call you my mother. We are no longer going to interact with each other. We need to find a psychiatrist for you. Who are you to ruin the royal traditions of Ayodhya? You have no right to send your son out into the jungles. You do not know how to be a mother. I love Mother Kaushalya and Mother Sumitra much more than you, you insane person. I am not going to accept the position which is legally Rama's. I am going to see Rama and Lakshmana at the forest." Bharata left angrily. Kaikeyi was really guilty about her action. Bharata walked by and saw Shatrughna hitting Manthara for he knew who was responsible for Kaikeyi's actions.

Bharata saw that and he asked Shatrughna, "Why are you hitting this woman? She wasn't responsible for anything."

Shatrughna replied, "This woman is responsible for all the bad events that took place in Ayodhya. She is the one who poisoned Kaikeyi's mind into asking father those two boons. She wanted you to become the king instead of Rama."

Bharata said, "Kaikeyi is the one who is responsible because she took the action. She caused father to be separated from Rama and she caused the death of father. Kaikeyi also lied by saying that she was in a bad mood. Rama is way superior to me and he is the only person in this kingdom who deserves the throne. I am going to visit Rama and Lakshmana with Mother Kaushalya, Mother Sumitra, Kaikeyi, and other citizens who want to see Rama." Bharata and Shatrughna grieved and grieved.

Bharata and Shatrughna visited Queen Kaushalya and Queen Sumitra. The two brothers could not bear to see their mothers cry like this. They were crying bitterly. Sage Vasishta tried to calm Bharata down but Bharata was uncontrollable. Bharata told his mothers that he does not want to take the throne that Rama deserves and he also said that he wants to see Rama, Lakshmana, and Seetha. The two queens accepted Bharata's proposal to see the exiled people and took their sons to their father's dead body that was covered with oil for two or three weeks. Bharata was grieving in front of his father. Bharata and Shatrughna cried so much that their eyes were burning. Vasishta performed Dasharatha's last rites and Bharata and Shatrughna sadly burned the body.

15. BHARATA MEETS RAMA

Bharata, Shatrughna, Kaikeyi, Kaushalya, and Sumitra, and other citizens, were on their way to see Rama, Lakshmana, and Seetha. Bharata took his brother's golden sandals along with him. Bharata met Guha on the way and he hugged Guha because he is Rama's friend. Guha told Bharata that Rama sleeps everyday on a bed of leaves and it is sad to watch a king lie down on a bed full of leaves. Guha also told Bharata that Rama is now at Sage Bharadwaja's ashram. When Bharata was there, he asked Sage Bharadwaja where Rama is and he said that Rama is at Chitrakuta. When Bharata was close to Chitrakuta, Lakshmana thought that Bharata would attack them. He also thought that Bharata is going to fight with them because he has an army of people (who actually do not want to attack them).

Lakshmana said, "I hereby vow that I should attack Bharata and his army!"

Suddenly, a voice from heaven said, "Beware Lakshmana! Your oath is terrible. Bharata is not going to hurt you!"

Bharata came to Rama and Lakshmana and said sadly, "Oh my dear brothers! How are you? I have very bad news for you."

Rama said, "Please tell us the bad news, Bharata."

Bharata, very sorrowful, said, "Our father is dead!" Rama's eyes were not blinking for a long time. It looked like he was unconscious and he looked like he was blind.

Rama said, "What? Father is dead? Oh my god! We are half-orphaned!" Lakshmana and Seetha cried as if Bharata cried when he saw his father's dead body. Kaushalya, Sumitra, and Kaikeyi were crying.

Kaikeyi said to Rama, "Please forgive me for my mistake. I was not responsible for my actions. I didn't know what I was doing and lied to Bharata."

Rama said, "You haven't made any mistake." They were all grieving. Bharata wanted to bring Rama back to Ayodhya but Rama objected because he did not want to disobey his father's command. The citizens were very sad to see Rama living like a poor person when he is supposed to rule the kingdom. Bharata was happy that he saw Rama but he was very sad for his father's death and the low class comfort of Rama's hermitage.

16. RAMA AT ATRI'S ASHRAM

After Bharata visited Rama, Seetha, and Lakshmana, the trio decided to leave Chitrakuta and see Sage Atri and his wife Anusuya. Rama and Lakshmana did a namaskaram and they said the abhivaadaye to Sage Atri. Anusuya was talking to Seetha about a woman's Dharma. She also had the time to teach Seetha a small veena lesson. Anusuya has white hair and she had a good character. Anusuya offered Seetha a boon but Seetha did not want a boon. Seetha was telling her life story to her. Sage Atri told Rama and Lakshmana to go to the Dandaka Forest.

On their way to the Dandaka Forest, the trio saw a rakshasa named Viradha. Viradha was a rakshasa who looked like an octopus. He was very arrogant and he says that no one can kill him due to Lord Brahma's boons. He is the son of Jaya and Shatharada. Rama killed him with his arrows. Rama later found out that he was a Gandharva named Tumburu who was cursed by Lord Kubera to assume the demon form. Rama went to Sage

Sharabhanga's ashram and he recited some mantras. Rama also went to Sage Sutheekshna's ashram and he talked about the different impressions of the Dandaka Forest. Rama later went to Sage Agastya's ashram where he spent time sleeping on a stone and talking about Dharma.

17. RAMA MEETS JATAYU

In the Panchavati Forest, the trio met an immense eagle.

Rama asked the eagle, "Who are you?"

The eagle replied, "Welcome! My name is Jatayu and I used to be King Dasharatha's friend. I am Garuda's nephew. My mother is Aruna and my father is Shyeni. This forest is dangerous so I will guard your wife Seetha whenever she is in danger. Rama embraced Jatayu because he was his father's friend. The Panchavati forest was filled with blue and yellow flowers. There were beautiful pink roses. Peacocks were dancing around. The mountains were steep. Lakshmana built an ashram near the Godavari River where Rama brought lotuses. Everyday, the trio said mantras in praise of all gods.

18. SHURPANAKA'S DESIRE

One day, a rakshasi named Shurpanaka flew over the trio's ashram. She saw Rama and she wanted to marry him. She thought Rama was handsome. She later dressed up as a princess and came to Rama. She asked Rama who he was and Rama asked her who she was.

Then Seetha came out and asked Rama, "Who is this lady?"

Rama replied, "Her name is Shurpanaka and she is Maricha's niece."

Shurpanaka asked Rama, "Can you marry me?"

Rama replied, "Sorry, I already have a wife who is right next to me. Ask Lakshmana, the man right next to you." Lakshmana refused to marry her.

46

Shurpanaka said, "This ugly lady is your wife? How outrageous! I want to eat her!" Seetha was very terrified and Lakshmana came out and cut her nose off. Shurpanaka again took the form of a rakshasi and went back to Lanka.

19. KHARA AND DUSHANA

Shurpanaka reached Lanka and she went to the court directly with her swollen nose.

She told her brothers Khara and Dushana, "Look at your injured sister. A man attacked me by cutting my nose. You are even superior to Lord Indra. Go and kill him."

Khara asked her, "Who are these men? I will cut them into pieces. Tell me how this happened."

Shurpanaka replied, "I was flying over the Panchavati Forest and I saw a man from above. I wanted to marry him since I thought he was handsome. The man was called Rama and he is the son of Dasharatha, the King of Ayodhya. I asked him if he could marry me but he said he already had one wife and he was not willing to take another. He told me to ask Lakshmana but the man Lakshmana refused. He realized that I was insulting Rama's wife and he cut off my nose and then I went back here to Lanka hastily."

Dushana said, "Who in the world would dare to insult our rakshasa clan? Don't they know that we are superior to every living creature in the world? I am going straight to the Panchavati forest with Khara to kill those two men."

Shurpanaka was very happy and she stayed back in Lanka. Khara and Dushana went to the Panchavati forest with their army. Rama and Lakshmana heard a voice and they saw a rakshasa army who wanted to kill them.

20. THE DEATH OF KHARA AND DUSHANA

The army said in a group, "Beware Rama and Lakshmana! You will get what you deserve for insulting my sister Shurpanaka! Challenge us to a fight if you both are prepared to die!"

Rama and Lakshmana replied, "We will fight against you. You shall die now." Rama told Lakshmana that he could fight by himself. Rama used his weapons and fought against the rakshasa army alone. In one arrow, he killed the whole rakshasa army.

21. RAVANA TO THE RESCUE

Meanwhile in Lanka, Shurpanaka heard of Khara and Dushana's death. She was so furious that she came up to her other brother Ravana who had ten heads. Ravana was shocked when he heard that Khara and Dushana died. Shurpanaka told Ravana about the beauty of Seetha. Ravana imagined how Seetha would look by listening to Shurpanaka's words. Shurpanaka told Ravana that Seetha was the wife of the man who killed Khara and Dushana. Ravana listened to Shurpanaka's words carefully. He wanted to marry Seetha but he decided to kidnap her because she was the wife of the man who murdered Khara and Dushana. Ravana thought that he could kidnap Seetha easily because he got many boons from Lord Shiva that nobody could kill him. Ravana decided to talk to Mandodari, his wife about his plan. Mandodari accepted the plan but she decided to give Seetha gifts after she married Ravana. Everybody accepted the plan except for Vibheeshana, Ravana's brother who was a man dedicated to Lord Shiva and Dharma. He thought that kidnapping a woman is against Dharma. He knew there was going to be a war for Seetha and he wanted to be on Rama's side because he knew what his brother would do is wrong. Ravana did not like Vibheeshana's advice.

22. RAVANA MEETS MAREECHA

Ravana first decided to go to his uncle Mareecha. He went to Mareecha's hut.

Ravana said, "Please accept my greetings, uncle."

Mareecha replied, "Ravana, what do you want?"

Ravana said, "I want to kidnap Seetha, the wife of Rama who is the son of Dasharatha, the king of Ayodhya because I want to take revenge on Rama's brother Lakshmana who cut off Shurpanaka's nose. I want you to listen to my instructions."

Mareecha said, "Shri Ram is very strong and it is not easy to kidnap his wife."

Ravana said, "Do you want me to kill you here or could you help me?"

Mareecha said, "Okay, I will help you."

Ravana said, "Go in the guise of a deer at the Panchavati forest. Rama will go after you because Seetha would want you. Rama will kill you and you call for Lakshmana in Rama's voice. Seetha will persuade Lakshmana to look what Rama was doing. When Lakshmana is gone, I will come to kidnap Seetha in the form of a sanyasi."

23. SEETHA KIDNAPPED

A few days later, Ravana flew in his Pushpak Aircraft with Mareecha to the Panchavati forest where they land and Mareecha transformed into a golden deer while Ravana hid in the bushes. Seetha saw the golden deer and asked Rama to get the deer for her. Rama took his arrow and shot the deer out of the jungle. The minute that the golden deer was shot by Rama, Mareecha yelled out, "Help me Lakshmana! Help me." Seetha thought that Rama was shot or killed and she persuaded Lakshmana to go where Rama was. Lakshmana drew a line which Seetha could not cross for safety reasons.

Later, Ravana changed his form to a sanyasi. He went to Seetha's ashram and he asked Seetha for some food. Seetha gave him food. The minute Seetha gave him food, Ravana snatched the food and threw it on the ground. Ravana crossed the line but Ravana was not affected when he crossed the line. He revealed his identity and kidnapped Seetha immediately in his Pushpak Aircraft. Once Ravana lifted the aircraft up to the sky, Seetha was throwing jewels to the ground and was yelling. Rama and Lakshmana could not hear. Seetha tried to convince Ravana to leave her alone but he did not.

"You idiot, who is never responsible for his actions, tell me who you are, where you are taking me, and why you are kidnapping me. You should be ruined, you sinner. I hate you!"

24. JATAYU DEAD

Jatayu heard Seetha and he wanted to save her. He went up to the sky and fought Ravana. Ravana cut off his wings and he fell to the ground.

Meanwhile, when Lakshmana reached the end of the jungles, Rama asked him, "I thought I told you to protect Seetha. Why did you come here?"

Lakshmana replied, "We heard you yelling and Seetha persuaded me to come here because she thought you were in danger."

Rama said, "That yelling was a trick from a rakshasa. The rakshasa made you believe that I was hurt but I wasn't. Now we can go back to Seetha." On the way, the two brothers saw Jatayu in a painful state. Rama asked Jatayu what happened.

Jatayu replied, "Ravana kidnapped Seetha. I tried to save Seetha but Ravana cut off my wings. Go towards the south." Then, Jatayu died. Rama and Lakshmana performed Jatayu's last rites.

25. THE SEARCH

Rama and Lakshmana met a rakshasa. His name was Kabandha. He said that Lord Indra and a rishi cursed him. He said that he lost his power of knowledge and that he had lost his feet. He was actually a man named Dhanu. He was very sorry for the kidnapping of Seetha.

Kabandha said, "There is a monkey by name Sugriva. His brother Vali has pushed him out of the kingdom. Vali rules Kishkindha. He has harassed Sugriva a lot. He might search for Seetha if you kill Vali but only do it when Sugriva tells you to. There is an old woman named Shabari. She was asked to go to heaven but when she heard that Lord Vishnu was coming into the Dandaka Forest as Rama, she refused to. She wanted to see Rama. She is still waiting for you. She has put flowers in front of God because she wishes that you would come. She has promised that she would go to heaven after seeing you. Go towards Pampasaras and you will see her ashram on the way." Rama said he would go.

Rama and Lakshmana went ahead towards Pampasaras. Meanwhile, Shabari, who had a high devotion to Rama which nobody could describe, set up dandelions right in front of God. People kept on telling her that Rama would never come but still she was not convinced. She finally saw Rama and she was very happy. She had a smile of about 6 inches long. Rama also spotted Shabari. Shabari quickly got some fruits and vegetables. She fed Rama and Lakshmana in her happiness. People were amazed that she was right.

Shabari asked Rama, "Oh my Lord! What do you want to eat? I am very happy to see you."

Rama replied, "My wife Seetha was kidnapped by a rakshasa named Ravana. I want to go to Kishkindha to see Sugriva. Please tell me how to get there."

Shabari said, "Go towards the mountain of Rishyamooka, the home of Kishkindha." Shabari was so happy.

Rama said, "I have to go right now."

Shabari said, "I have taken a vow that I would go to heaven with my guru after I saw you. Oh Lord, may you be strong all the time." Rama gave her a good blessing. Shabari said some last words and suddenly vanished.

After the incident at Shabari's ashram, Rama was busy grieving about Seetha's disappearance. Lakshmana kept quiet and was also guilty because he didn't protect Seetha well. Both of them walked toward the mountain of Rishyamooka. Lakshmana was very quiet and Rama was grieving and he was saying, "I can't live without Seetha and we have to find her quickly!"

Lakshmana said, "We have to go quickly. I feel very guilty because I was not careful enough."

Rama said, "There is no need for you to feel guilty. It is Ravana's fault and he will soon be torn up into pieces." They reached Rishyamooka after a while.

Sugriva saw both of them. He saw two men walking near the mountain. He thought those two men were sent by Vali to kill him. He got suspicious and sent his servant Hanuman to the men (who were actually Rama and Lakshmana). Hanuman was a big monkey known for his intelligence and power. He was actually born to serve Rama. He was the son of Vayu and

Girish Rathnam Swaminath

the son of Anjana. He approached Rama and Lakshmana to find out who they were under Sugriva's command.

26. RAMA MEETS SUGRIVA

Hanuman asked Rama and Lakshmana, "Who are you? I have been sent by Sugriva to find out who you are."

Rama replied, "My name is Rama and right next to me is my brother Lakshmana. We are both princes of Ayodhya. My wife has been kidnapped by a rakshasa named Ravana. I wanted to talk to Sugriva about this."

Hanuman replied, "I will take you two to Sugriva. Please follow me."

When the three people reached Sugriva, Hanuman said, "The two men seek your friendship and they have not come to attack us. Those men are the princes of Ayodhya." Sugriva was relieved that the men did not come to attack them.

Sugriva said, "Please call them."

Rama said, "Please accept my greetings. My name is Rama and next to me is my brother Lakshmana. We are both princes of Ayodhya. Please accept my friendship."

Sugriva said, "Please sit down. What is it that you want to discuss about?" Rama said, "My wife Seetha has been kidnapped by this rakshasa named Ravana. My mother told us to go to the Dandaka Forest for fourteen years. Could you please help me to find Seetha, my wife who is kidnapped by the rakshasa Ravana?"

Sugriva replied, "I have some jewels that a woman threw from the air. It might be Seetha's. Yes, if you help me do something. My brother Vali has been harassing me. He banished me from the kingdom. He is causing trouble. He kidnapped my wife. Vali is so mean to me. Could you please kill him? I will let you stay here." Rama said, "Yes, I will kill him." Sugriva replied, "I first want to tell you how Vali's harassing me. One day, Vali fought with a rakshasa inside a cave. Vali told me to wait outside the caves. I suddenly heard a sound and I thought that Vali was dead. Actually, the rakshasa died. I did not want the rakshasa to eat me so I used a rock to close the cave's entrance and exit. I notified everybody at Kishkindha's palace that Vali was dead. Then my pattabishekam happened. Suddenly Vali came. He said that I was nothing but a man who is jealous of his own brother. He also hurt my feelings. To take revenge, he kidnapped my wife."

27. VALI DEAD

Vali was very anxious to fight against Sugriva. But his son Angada and his wife Tara worried about him. Sugriva was fighting against Vali later on. They were going through a terrible fight. Their gold maces had turned brown in fighting. Rama was anxious to kill Vali. Rama thought, "The fight has been taking too long and I better kill Vali right now." Rama decided to hide behind a tree and shoot Vali with his arrows. Rama pulled the bow to shoot Vali and he suddenly released the arrow which hit Vali. Vali was in absolute pain. He was lucky to be alive in the last two hours. Vali realized that Rama was God. He begged for forgiveness and he could not believe that he was dying right in front of god. Sugriva and Rama tried taking off the arrow but they could not. Sugriva was also sad and happy. He was asking for forgiveness over and over and he praised Rama several times. Meanwhile, Tara and Angada came to see Vali. Tara and Angada were crying crazily. Vali promised that Sugriva can ascend the throne and be the King of Kishkindha. Rama tried to calm Vali down and talk to him. Vali suddenly died. Tara was very sad and could not be comforted.

After the death of Vali, Rama and Lakshmana decided to arrange for the coronation of Sugriva as King of Kishkindha and Angada as Prince of Kishkindha. Sugriva was crowned king after he reunited with his wife. The city was full of lights when the coronation happened. Angada was crowned prince.

28. LAKSHMANA VERY FURIOUS

Rama returned to Kishkindha with Lakshmana, Sugriva, and others. Rama asked Sugriva to send Angada and his army to search for Seetha. Sugriva said, "I will send Angada and his army to look for Seetha. We will have to look in the South." Sugriva later was having some fun before taking care of Seetha's search. He was drunk. He did not obey any other monkey. Lakshmana later saw that Sugriva was drunk and he was furious. Angada saw Lakshmana come and he wanted to guard Sugriva's room so he could not see what was happening. Nevertheless, Lakshmana already saw what was happening.

Angada came and said, "Your Honor, what do you want?"

Lakshmana replied furiously, "I want to see Sugriva now!" Angada let him in. Lakshmana entered the palace and heard music and the strings of the veena. He also saw beautiful women.

Lakshmana said, "When are you going to send the army to the South? When are you going to take action? You know what, Rama has not been able to sleep and you are just enjoying?"

Hanuman said, "Oh King, what you have been doing is wrong. You are not following Dharma and you are not being helpful. Stop having fun and let's discuss how to find Seetha." Sugriva kept quiet and he realized his mistake. He asked for forgiveness. Lakshmana was calmed and he asked for forgiveness.

Sugriva told Angada, "Please go with your army to the south and search for Seetha. I want all the arrangements done before ten days." They agreed. Before leaving, Rama gave his ring to Hanuman just in case.

Angada and his army searched everywhere for Seetha, in the mountains, in the caves, and in every place. Nevertheless, they had no luck. They were finally at the beach where they were near the mountains.

Angada discussed with Hanuman and the other group members, "Sugriva gave us only one month's time and three months have already passed. I know that it is wrong to disobey Sugriva but our mission is to look for Seetha or else Sugriva might give us a death penalty."

29. ARMY MEETS SAMPATI

When the group was deliberating, they saw an eagle called Sampati. He was the brother of Jatayu. He lived in a small cave filled with rocks at the coast. He was orangish-yellow and he had a very big smile. When Seetha was kidnapped, he saw Ravana kidnapping her and he knew that Ravana was going to Lanka.

The group asked Sampati, "What is your name? Who are you? Hello, Sugriva, the King of Kishkindha, sent us to look for a woman named Seetha. She is the wife of Rama, from Ayodhya, and she is the daughter of Janaka, the ruler of Mithila. She was kidnapped by a rakshasa named Ravana. Do you know where he is?"

Sampati replied in his low voice, "I saw the rakshasa Ravana with a woman. He rules Lanka and I am sure that Seetha is in Lanka. You have to cross many kilometers of the sea."

Angada said, "Thank you for telling us this information. May you be prosperous and live for millions of years." Then Sampati flew away. Sampati was God to the group because he told them very important news.

After Sampati flew away, the group decided for Hanuman to go to Lanka himself but Hanuman said that he did not have the powers to fly over the see to go to Lanka. Neela, one of the ministers, reminded Hanuman of a curse. When Hanuman was young, a rishi was meditating. Hanuman was jumping up and down and that caused the rishi to go up and down. The rishi was so angry that he wanted to curse Hanuman. The rishi cursed Hanuman, "You will lose all your powers. You will also forget that you have had powers before this curse!" Anjana, Hanuman's mother, begged for forgiveness but the rishi did not listen to her. The only thing that the rishi did to satisfy Anjana was that if anybody reminded of the curse after a decade later, Hanuman will start to remember his powers. So the minister reminded Hanuman about the curse. Then Hanuman realized that he could fly and do many other things. He blessed the other minister a lot and he was very happy when he heard about his powers.

30. HANUMAN AT LANKA

Hanuman departed the coast. He was flying over bluish-green waters. The waves were very high. Hanuman came across much distraction in the air and they were all rakshasas. He always had an explanation for the rakshasas to leave him alone. Finally, Hanuman reached Lanka. It was a broad, populated island. People were crowding around in the streets. People were arrogant due to their leader Ravana. Millions of people had died because of him. When Hanuman reached Lanka, he changed his size to a mouse's size and he came to Lanka. He saw a huge rakshasi who was guarding the palace of Lanka. She was sleeping and Hanuman wanted to sneak above her. But the rakshasi woke up and was threatening to eat him. Hanuman got really scared and he told her that he wanted to see Ravana. Then she let him in. Hanuman, in his small size, flew and saw Vibheeshana. He was scared. Then when Hanuman heard Vibheeshana saying the words "Shri Ram," he turned to his normal size. They had a friendly conversation. Vibheeshana told Hanuman that he wanted to join Rama's side. Hanuman was shocked that somebody says Shri Ram in Lanka. Later, Hanuman turned to his mouse size. He flew over Ravana and Mandodari.

Later, Hanuman reached Ashokavana, a garden in Lanka which had many fruits. Hanuman saw Seetha over there. Some rakshasis were threatening Seetha that Ravana would marry her but Seetha believed that Rama would come to Lanka and kill Ravana. Her days have passed by grieving. All the rakshasis were threatening Seetha that she would be killed if she does not accept Ravana.

All the rakshasis were asleep but Seetha was not. She was busy grieving and remembering the days she was with Rama. Hanuman saw Seetha later at Ashokavana, which is a grassland filled with plants, fruits, and vegetables. Five rakshasis who were asleep were supposed to guard Seetha. Seetha was very sad and Hanuman could notice that.

31. HANUMAN MEETS SEETHA

Hanuman came to Seetha and he said, "Pranams to you Devi. I am your messenger. I have been sent here by your beloved husband Rama."

Seetha said, "How do you prove that you were sent by my husband Rama?"

Hanuman replied, "Here is your husband's ring and he gave this to me to say that I have been sent by him. Anyway, now I will tell you the story of how Rama and Lakshmana came looking for you. At Panchavati, when you were kidnapped, it was not Rama who yelled. The deer actually was Mareecha, the uncle of Ravana. Rama talked to the king Sugriva about you and he asked for help. First, Rama killed Vali following Sugriva's command. Sugriva later sent an army with me and other monkeys. We were at the coastline and we saw an eagle called Sampati, who was the brother of Jatayu who is a vulture. He saw Ravana kidnap you. Therefore, he told us how to go to Lanka. One of the monkeys told me about a curse that forced me to forget my powers. Then I was reminded of my powers and I flew to Lanka over the sea."

Seetha said, "May God bless you. You are so lucky to have an intelligent mind. You are the correct follower of Dharma. You are so humble to people and you are clever. I will give you a part of my salwar to give to you. Also take the salwar piece to prove to my lord that you saw me. Oh No! Watch out! Hide behind the trees! Ravana is coming!" Hanuman took a bunch of fruits and ate them after he hid behind one of the trees.

Ravana came to Seetha and said, "If you don't accept me, you shall die." Ravana and many other women threatened Seetha. After the blackmailing of the rakshasis and Ravana, Hanuman came out and decided to take revenge.

32. AKSHAY KUMAR DEAD

After Ravana and the others left, Hanuman destroyed the gardens of Ashokavana and one of the guards saw Hanuman. Immediately, the guard reported to Ravana that a monkey destroyed Ashokavana.

Ravana exclaimed, "A monkey! Akshay Kumar, go and capture him." Akshay Kumar went to Ashokavana and saw Hanuman.

Akshay Kumar yelled, "Beware you little monkey! I am Akshay Kumar, the son of the Maha Rakshasa, Ravana! I am superior to Lord Indra. I will crush you into pieces. Ha Ha Ha Ha Ha Ha Ha Ha Ha Ha Ha!"

Hanuman was scared and said, "Let's handle this over a talk."

Akshay Kumar pretended as if he did not hear Hanuman and they started fighting. It was just an arrow war. Akshay Kumar shot many arrows at Hanuman but Hanuman dodged all of them. Hanuman shot an arrow at Akshay Kumar and missed him. Hanuman later got into a fist fight with Akshay Kumar and shot another arrow at Akshay Kumar. Hanuman's arrow hit Akshay Kumar and he fell to the ground.

Akshay Kumar told Hanuman, "You sinner, you will never get away with this. If I lose, then somebody would take my place and kill you!" Akshay Kumar fell dead after he said his last words.

All the guards ran crying and yelling, "A rakshasa beaten by a monkey! Outrageous!"

Ravana heard the guards yelling and said, "What do you mean?" One of the guards said, " Akshay Kumar is dead! He was beaten by that outrageous monkey." Ravana was extremely sad about his son's death. However, he wanted Hanuman to be killed.

Ravana yelled, "Indrajit, go and capture that idiotic monkey that killed Akshay Kumar!" Indrajit immediately went to Ashokavana to find Hanuman. Indrajit saw Hanuman and told him, "Beware, monkey! You will be captured!"

33. HANUMAN CAPTURED

Indrajit took a rope and kept on whipping Hanuman. Then he tied a rope around Hanuman. After tying the rope, Indrajit stopped whipping Hanuman. Hanuman was very angry at the fact that he was treated as a slave. He was really angry and his face became red.

Indrajit took poor Hanuman to the court of Ravana. Ravana had a red face when he saw Hanuman. Ravana said, "We rakshasas are so powerful that we could even kill all the gods. Try to kill us and you shall die. Now, you are going to be sentenced to a death penalty. Indrajit, go and burn this monkey's tail." Hanuman was not given time to say another word and in one second his tail was burnt. Suddenly, Hanuman loosened the ropes and lengthened his tail. He flew to the ceiling of the palace and made a hole with his powerful physical abilities. Hanuman flew to the sky and burned Lanka. A populated area with lots of houses and busy palaces has now become a deserted and homeless area. Almost all the people living in Lanka died. Many children died or at least were injured. It was a sad and hopeless day for Lanka and its people. The only section of Lanka that Hanuman left alone was Ashokavana because of Seetha. After burning everything, Hanuman dipped his tail into the sea to make his tail cool down. Meanwhile, Hanuman decided that it is too dangerous to stay at Lanka any longer and also thought that this was the time to see Rama. Before Hanuman left to the coast, Vibheeshana told Hanuman he wanted to side with Rama.

The next day, Hanuman flew back to the shore using his super powers. When Hanuman flew to Lanka, he had come across many obstructions. Since he was flying away from Lanka now, the obstructions that he had crossed before were not obstructing him now. Hanuman had amazing thoughts about what Seetha said to him and his victories at Lanka. By the time he had finished thinking, he reached the coast and did not even know it. He was not paying attention to where he was going. He was paying attention to the events that happened in Lanka. Suddenly, Hanuman realized that he was going to crash into a huge sand dune. He made a sharp turn and...Wham! He ran into Angada's army.

Angada said, "Hanuman, you could have paid attention as to where you were going. Anyway, did you find Seetha? What happened in Lanka?"

Hanuman replied, "Let us go towards Kishkindha and I will tell you the story. I crossed many rakshasas and rakshasis when I was flying to Lanka. They all threatened to eat me but I lied to them so they let me go. When I came to Lanka, Vibheeshana, Ravana's brother, was the first person to whom I talked. He was one of the only people in Lanka who would say Shri Rama everyday. I went to Ashokavana (a vegetable garden) later that day and I saw Seetha over there. I told her about how Rama and Lakshmana came searching for her. She was depressed for all the rakshasis and Ravana were threatening her death. I also heard Ravana threaten Seetha and I did not like the way she was tortured by Ravana so I wanted to take revenge. I started to ruin Ashokavana and some guards saw me. They reported to Ravana saying that a monkey destroyed Ashokavana and Ravana immediately sent his arrogant, powerful son Akshay Kumar. He was just wasting time bragging that he is more powerful than Lord Indra. He started attacking me and I almost died. Afterwards, I shot plenty of arrows at Akshay Kumar and I finally killed him. The guards who were watching the fight ran to Ravana and after hearing that I had killed Akshay Kumar, he sent Indrajit, his other son, to capture me. I was captured and treated as a slave. Ravana decided that my tail should be burned and burnt it. Then I lengthened my tail and burned every part of Lanka except for Ashokavana. I thought that it wasn't safe for me at Lanka anymore so I came back here and also Ravana's brother Vibheeshana wants to side with us. I think he is a man of trustworthiness but I don't like the idea of having our enemy's brother in our camp."

34. PREPARATIONS FOR WAR

By the time Hanuman finished talking to the army about his journey, the army had reached Kishkindha and saw Sugriva and Rama outside. Rama asked, "Did you have any luck?"

Hanuman replied, "I will tell you everything that happened after we get in the palace." After getting into the palace, Hanuman told Rama everything that happened in his journey for searching for Seetha. Rama was crying when he heard that Hanuman met Seetha. He couldn't stand the fact that he was away from Seetha.

Rama said, "Hanuman, I couldn't have done anything without you. I do not know how to pay you back. Oh here, I have some gold for the army." The whole army was happy because Rama was happy and because they got the gold. There was a few minutes of silence after all this. Rama suddenly said, "We have to go to war and kill Ravana. I also think that we have to side with Ravana's brother Vibheeshana. He knows a lot about Dharma and is trustworthy. Even though he is the brother of Ravana, he is required for our army. We will train ourselves for the next two months. Lakshmana and I will tell you how to train and what to do. We will not take any action for a few months. All of you will have to come to the meeting, no excuses however. I am vowing that I shall kill Ravana before I go back to Ayodhya!"

After this event, Rama and Lakshmana helped the monkeys train. Rama hung a target and many monkeys shot arrows at the targets. Many monkeys made the target. Rama was so proud that he was fortunate to have a good army. After a day's training session, Hanuman said, "I know that we have a good army but it is impossible to kill Ravana. He has one thousand heads and after we shoot each head one head comes back."

Rama replied, "Courage, confidence, responsibility, and determination are some of the factors that you should have as a team. If we have these qualities, then by Lord Shiva's grace, we will succeed. According to Dharma, we should never give up and if we have a good reason to kill somebody, then we should keep that goal. You should always have a goal in life. No matter what people say about you, it is what you care that matters. Although Ravana is not an ordinary rakshasa, we can still kill him according to Dharma. We should work as a team and have good military strategies."

Angada said, "Oh Rama, you aren't a human, you are the eternal Lord Vishnu. You have memorized everything in Dharma and you are applying the principles of Dharma to your daily life. We do not know how to pay you back for you leading us to good Dharma. Dharma is our total acquisition. We have chosen to adhere to your plans. You have definitely increased our dedication to this war." After the training, the army went back to Kishkindha and had a good night's sleep.

The military training was everyday, mornings and evenings. The army was busy and they even practiced when there was not any army training. Rama split the army into two groups: the Ramachandra Nama and the Lakshmana Nama. The Ramachandra Nama was led by Rama and they helped the Lakshmana Nama physically. The Lakshmana Nama spent time on mental training and helped the Ramachandra Nama mentally. The main reason for these two groups was to help each other and to prepare the soldiers for war. There was a break only after a month and that was a huge celebration. They sang bhajans and enjoyed. They prayed to God and had fun eating good food. Rama became very sad when the first party came. He was reminded of Seetha and Rama suddenly started crying. Rama had lost his confidence but after the influencing of the monkeys and Lakshmana, he had regained his confidence.

After six months of training, Rama held a meeting. In the meeting, he said, "This is the most important meeting that we have ever had. Tomorrow we are going to start our journey to Lanka and there will be no more Ramachandra Nama and Lakshmana Nama. It is requisite to perform a pooja. We will start the pooja in another twenty minutes. When we do the pooja, we will have approval from the Devas about killing Ravana. This will also make us calm, powerful, and spiritual. We are going to say every sloka that we know today." After twenty minutes, the army started the pooja and chanted all the prayers they knew.

After the day of prayer, all of the army's members stood in a line at Kishkindha. They were ready to go to war. Rama made sure everybody was there and everybody was there.

Rama yelled out, "Some of you might not be able to hear me now. This is our first step. Lakshmana will give instructions to those in the back and I will for those in the front. Take some soil on your right hand and throw it up. As you throw it up, say the Gayathri Mantra out loud. As you say the Gayathri Mantra, you close your eyes and take a step forward."

The fighters took the step and received spiritual powers. The army passed jungles and forests which had many animals. The animals were wild and the army was also threatened by a few. There were many poisonous snakes and crocodiles. The soldiers all had to sleep on something that was known as a "dust bed." The dust bed was like a bed made of dust that was believed to be carved by erosion. Nothing seemed tenuous to the army and those who saw them walking towards Lanka. On the way, Rama saw a person from the village who lost both of his arms. After Rama saw the man, the man became ambidextrous. They crossed the poorest areas of Bharat and the journey took one month.

When the army reached the coast, they spent one hour of thinking how to cross the sea. Rama suddenly thought of an idea and told the army, "Everybody, please bring the amount of rocks that will be enough for crossing four hundred leagues of sea and bring the rocks to me." Therefore, the army brought Rama the rocks and Rama put the rocks on the ground one by one. Everybody followed Rama and the army crossed the sea successfully.

When the army reached Lanka in the morning, a rakshasa saw the army walking into Lanka and told Ravana about this. Ravana was shocked and furious. His calmness turned into anger.

Ravana said, "Oh, they want Seetha back. They won't get her back. It doesn't matter whether the three worlds face me but I WON'T GIVE SEETHA BACK! You two will get a death penalty tomorrow."

35. RAMA MEETS VIBHEESHANA

After two hours, Rama made a secret trip to Vibheeshana's palace and talked to Vibheeshana. Once he came inside the palace, he said, "Hello, my name is Rama and I am the Prince of Ayodhya. Your brother Ravana has kidnapped my wife Seetha and I have come to wage war against Ravana. About a few months ago, a monkey named Hanuman burned Lanka. Hanuman is a soldier of our army. He has come here to Lanka too and has told me about your good qualities. I believe that you should join my army."

Vibheeshana replied, "Oh Rama, you are the lotus of Lord Vishnu. I swear to all the gods in the universe and to Dharma that I will join your army and I will not betray your army of any kind. My brother should be ashamed of kidnapping somebody else's wife. I am ashamed to call him my brother." Rama dug a secret tunnel to the army camp and went through it with Vibheeshana.

During the next day, Ravana sent two rakshasas called Suka and Sarana to spy for the rakshasas. When the rakshasas went to Rama's army, Vibheeshana found out that those rakshasas were Ravana's spies. Vibheeshana was about to kill them but the rakshasas surrendered. Rama told the rakshasas to tell Ravana the following message, "Ravana, you don't know how my unbearable wrath is and tomorrow, I will destroy Lanka with one arrow. Savudhaan!"

One day later, the rakshasas told Ravana the message and Ravana was furious with them. He decided to kill them. After the death of the two rakshasas, Ravana wanted to cheat Seetha saying that Rama has been killed by him. So he started making a dummy that looked like Rama. After he made the dummy with blood and an arrow, he showed it to Seetha. Seetha believed Ravana and started to cry.

Seetha cried, "Rama, so brave and handsome got killed by this two-timer fool who doesn't know what he is doing. Wait a minute, I see Rama. That means that this rakshasa was trying to make me accept him and cheat me. I am going to punch this rakshasa now." So Seetha punched Ravana.

Ravana replied, "You have insulted my rakshasahood. After I marry you, you will be against Rama."

Seetha yelled, "Shut up. It is none of your business. You have no right to say such things. I have a right and I have chosen Rama as my husband, not you. Shut up and die a horrible death. None of the Devas are going to save you now. Anyway, go and mind your own business. I am not listening to a word you say nor will I reply. Get out of Ashokavana and go back to your palace. Your wife Mandodari is okay and you should be content with her."

36. THE WAR

After Ravana's failed attempt of cheating Seetha, Rama's army started the war. The army started to break open the gates of Lanka. All the people were running away and most of the people had to commit suicide by drowning themselves. As the people were committing suicide, Ravana's army came out of the palace to defend Lanka. Many soldiers were killed and there was so much blood that the blood entered the sea. Ravana was just lazy thinking that the rakshasas will win the war. Indrajit fought against Angada and both of them were equally powerful so the fight was interesting to watch. Hanuman fought against Rajkumar while Rama fought with four rakshasas at a time. Sriman was killed by Lakshmana with one arrow. All the chariots of Ravana were crushed by Rama's army but nobody cared.

During the war, Rama said, "Savudhaan! Indrajit is the son of Ravana who has gotten boons from Lord Brahma and was born to destroy the three worlds. I will take care of him."

So Rama fought Indrajit but Indrajit used a weapon that made Rama and Lakshmana faint. Seetha saw them and thought that they were dead but one of the rakshasis who felt sorry for Seetha told her that Rama isn't dead and she gave some proof.

Rama was still lying on the ground. Vibheeshana sprinkled some water on top of Rama and said some mantras. Immediately, Rama woke up. Rama saw Lakshmana and was in tears. Vibheeshana contacted Sushena, a physician. Sushena examined Lakshmana.

Sushena said, "Lakshmana is unconscious and I think Vayu's son Hanuman should go and get two herbs: the Sanjeevani and the Vishalyani from the ocean of milk. Hanuman has to come back with the herbs before sunset if Lakshmana has to live."

The minute Sushena said that, Hanuman left to the ocean of milk and got a forest of the Sanjeevani and the Vishalyani herbs. Hanuman carried the whole mountain and put the herbs near Lakshmana's nose. Lakshmana sniffed the herbs and woke up.

Everybody in Lanka found out that Lakshmana was cured. When the news reached Ravana, Ravana became furious. He sent a powerful rakshasa named Dharmayuddha who brought a huge army. Hanuman fought Dharmayuddha.

Hanuman said, "Savudhaan Dharmayuddha! You will die. Who gave you the name Dharmayuddha anyway, you loser?"

Dharmayuddha could not stand that insult and he was going to reply to Hanuman but was killed before saying anything. Ravana sent Varadaraja after the death of Dharmayuddha and Varadaraja was killed by Angada. Ankalampana was sent after Varadaraja but was killed by Hanuman. Ravana was so depressed to find his greatest warriors lying on the ground. He later sent Prahastha, his commander-in-chief. Neela threw a large rock on Prahastha and punched him and killed Prahastha.

Ravana was so furious that he entered the battlefield to arrange the army so he could catch the attention of Rama's army. Hanuman saw Ravana and told him that he was Akshay Kumar's murderer. Ravana was smiling and then punched Hanuman on the back. Hanuman dodged it.

Hanuman said, "Let's see who is better: the humble one or the arrogant one." Hanuman shot Dharmayuddha.

37. KUMBHAKARNA TO THE RESCUE

Ravana's only hope was Kumbhakarna, his son who was the strongest rakshasa after Ravana. Ravana had to rely on Kumbhakarna because all of his strong rakshasas died. Kumbhakarna was asleep and Ravana tried to wake him up.

"Hello Kumbhakarna! Could you hear me? How could you sleep while watching all of our warriors die. You are my only hope! Come on!

Ravana tried his best but Kumbhakarna did not get up. Ravana got some water and poured it on Kumbhakarna. Kumbhakarna woke up and said, "Father, why did you wake me up?"

"Kumbhakarna, don't ask any questions and pressure me. Go dress up and go to the battlefield. You are my only hope. All the other rakshasas that are trained have died."

Kumbhakarna dressed up and his chain was sparkling white. He wore a yellow dress and a brown pant. He went to the battlefield with a brave personality. When he entered the battlefield, a huge light was shining on him. Sugriva saw Kumbhakarna and started to praise him but Kumbhakarna thought that he was sarcastic. Therefore, Kumbhakarna pulled Sugriva's shirt and a wrestling match was started. Kumbhakarna was killed after Sugriva punched Kumbhakarna inside the eye.

Seeing that Kumbhakarna died, Indrajit became sad and he started to cry. Lakshmana approached him and said, "Savudhaan Indrajit! It does not matter if you are superior to all the Devas in the universe. You will die and will be killed by me."

Indrajit said, "Lakshmana, Lakshmana, Lakshmana! You don't get it, do you? You don't know how to fight, do you? Well I can destroy this army with one weapon and this was given by Lord Brahma."

While Indrajit was taking out the Brahmastra, Lakshmana took his mace and hit Indrajit on the head three times. Indrajit died and all the

Girish Rathnam Swaminath

rakshasas in the battlefield stopped fighting. Lord Indra came down from heaven and told Lakshmana, "Oh great warrior! Oh Mahatma! You have killed Indrajit, a really powerful rakshasa. Not even the Devas could kill him. You deserve my chariot and Ravana will be killed by Rama."

"Pranams to you, Lord! I cannot accept this award. My brother Rama is better than me and deserves this more than me. Please give this chariot to him."

Therefore, Lord Indra approached Rama and gave him the chariot. All the rakshasas were shocked and Ravana was so furious that he felt like committing suicide. All of his sons were dead and this was the unfortunate time for Ravana.

Ravana could hardly sleep and he was thinking about what to do in the war. He was having nightmares that he died and that Rama liberated Seetha. Ravana thought that he could enter the battlefield himself. That sounded like a good idea to him but will it work?

38. RAVANA DEAD

Ravana woke up at four in the morning and he started to get his sword and dressed up. At six o'clock, when the soldiers of Rama's army were ready to fight, Ravana entered the battlefield. The soldiers of Rama's army dropped their swords in shock and one soldier died because the sword landed on his foot.

Ravana yelled, "Savudhaan, in one arrow, I could kill all of you. Surrender or else!"

Rama said, "I will kill your stupid rakshasa army with one arrow. Start to fight. I don't think you would because you are too scared to fight."

The war started and Rama attacked Ravana. No matter how much times Rama attacked Ravana's heads, they kept on growing back in one

Girish Rathnam Swaminath

second. Rama shot Ravana's heads for eighteen days, day and night. After eighteen days, Rama became very impatient.

Rama asked Vibheeshana, "Oh King of Dharma! I have been shooting Ravana's heads for eighteen days but yet they grow back in one second. How can you kill all of Ravana's heads without them growing back?"

Vibheeshana replied, "Oh Lord! You have to shoot Ravana's navel and then you could kill him."

Hence, Rama aimed for Ravana's navel and Ravana died. The three worlds were shocked and all the gods were shocked. The war was all over. Now Rama can take Seetha back to Ayodhya. The soldiers could go back to Kishkindha. The army was very happy. Rama wanted to make Vibheeshana the king of Lanka. There was a huge coronation ceremony. There were red lights and many people. There was dancing, music, and other entertainment. Rama was so happy to see Seetha.

Seetha said, "Oh Rama! You killed Ravana--a two-timer thief. I cannot believe that you killed him. I should be lucky to have such a brave and intelligent husband, helpful monkeys, and a consoling brother-in-law. Hanuman was so brave and he is the King of Dharma. Vibheeshana made a right decision to oppose his brother Ravana. Sugriva is a very calm and confident man. I will be so sad to leave all of you. Goodbye!"

Rama said, "I am so happy to see you safe. I will get you anything you want. Let us go back to Ayodhya tomorrow."

Rama was sad to leave these great warriors. The next day, the army took Ravana's Pushpak Aircraft and flew to Kishkindha.

Hanuman said sadly, "I will be so sad to depart from you my Lord. I was born to serve you. I don't know how I can be separated from you. I will be sad to be separated from Seetha, Lakshmana, Sugriva, and Vibheeshana. Unfortunately, I will have to go back to heaven to see my parents and the other Devas. Goodbye."

Vibheeshana said, "There is no way to pay you back for making me King of Lanka. I will be very sad to see you leave."

Sugriva said, "I cannot leave you, Your Honor! It was a really big accomplishment that you killed Ravana. I shall remain devoted to you always.

39. THE END OF THE RAMAYANA

Rama, Seetha, and Lakshmana waved goodbye. They flew to Ayodhya. When they landed in Ayodhya. Kaikeyi, Kaushalya, and Sumitra welcomed Rama, Lakshmana, and Seetha. They had actually arranged a surprise party. Rama was going to be crowned king and there was a huge celebration. Seetha was crowned queen and Lakshmana was crowned prince. After a few years, Seetha gave birth to two sons: Lava and Kusha. The family lived happily ever after all. Seetha and Rama went back to heaven.

SRI RAAMA RAAMA RAMETI RAME RAAME MANORAMEY SAHASRANAAMA THATHULYAM RAAMA RAAMA VARAARAMEY!

FOREWORD

The Ramayana is a great epic known by everyone today. People learn more about Dharma and lessons of life. They learn about bravery, love, knowledge, and wealth. Whoever reads this will be prosperous in life. Their sins will be removed. They will learn more about ancient times and what role God plays in our world. He kills people, He rewards people, and He does much more.

GLOSSARY

1. Lord Vishnu- A god with four hands. He holds a conch shell or sankha indicating spread of the divine sound "Om," he holds a discus or chakra, a reminder of the wheel of time and to lead a good life, he holds a lotus or Padma which is an example of glorious existence, and he holds a mace or gada which indicates the power and the punishing capacity of the Lord if discipline in life is ignored. His vehicle is the bird Garuda which can spread the Vedic knowledge with great courage. He rests on the bed of the powerful, coiled serpent, Seshnag. Lord Vishnu's consort is Goddess Lakshmi, the Goddess of Wealth.

2. Goddess Lakshmi- Goddess of Wealth, Prosperity, Purity, and Generosity. Her four hands represent four spiritual virtues. She sits on a fully blossomed lotus, a seat of divine truth. She has divine happiness, mental and spiritual satisfaction, and prosperity.

3. Lord Brahma- The creator God of the Universe. He is seated on a lotus, a symbol of glorious existence. He has four heads and hands. Each hand is holding a sacrificial tool, the Vedas (knowledge), a water pot, and a pink rose. His vehicle is a swan which is known for its judgment between good and bad.

4. Ravana- Rakshasa or demon who kidnapped Seetha. He was killed by Rama.

5. Ayodhya- Lord Rama's birthplace. It was the capital city of the Kosala kingdom.

6. King Dasharatha- Father of Rama and King of Ayodhya. He died of sorrow because he was separated from Rama.

7. Kaushalya- Mother of Rama and eldest wife of Dasharatha.

8. Sumitra- Wife of Dasharatha and mother of Lakshmana and Shatrughna.

9. Kaikeyi- Wife of Dasharatha and mother of Bharata. She made Rama, Lakshmana, and Seetha go to the forest for fourteen years.

10. Lord Agni- God of Fire who blessed Dasharatha with children by a yagna (pooja).

11. Payasam- A milk sweet. Kaushalya, Sumitra, and Kaikeyi drank this sweet and got children.

12. Rama- Dasharatha and Kaushalya's son and avatharam of Lord Vishnu.

13. Avatharam- Incarnation of a god. There are ten avatharams of Lord Vishnu: Matsya, Koorma, Varaha, Narasimha, Vamana, Parashurama, Balarama, Rama, Krishna, and Kalki.

14. Lakshmana- Dasharatha's and Sumitra's son.

15. Bharata- Dasharatha and Kaikeyi's son.

16. Shatrughna- Dasharatha and Sumitra's son.

17. Upanayanam- Function for entering adulthood.

18. Kulaguru- Teacher.

19. Poonal- Sacred thread that you get in your Upanayanam.

20. Sage Vishwamitra- Kulaguru of Dasharatha's sons.

21. Tataka- Rakshasi (demoness) who was the mother of Mareecha and Subahu and was killed by Rama.

22. Mareecha- Uncle of Ravana who was killed by Rama.

23. Subahu- Brother of Mareecha.

24. Sage Gautama- Great Sage.

25. Lord Indra- Lord of the Devas and Lord of Rain.

26. Swayamvara- Occasion where princess of a kingdom chooses her husband among the princes in the king's court.

27. Seetha- Wife of Rama and Daughter of Janaka.

28. Mithila- Capital city of the country Videha.

29. King Janaka- Ruler of Mithila and father of Seetha.

30. Bow of Mahadeva- Lord Shiva's bow.

31. Sage Parashurama- Great Sage who is the avatharam of Vishnu.

32. Sumantha- Dasharatha's charioteer.

33. Urmila- Lakshmana's wife.

34. Madhavi- Bharata's wife.

35. Srutakriti- Shatrughna's wife.

36. Saree- Women's clothing.

37. Veshti- Man's clothing.

38. Golusu- Type of Silver Jewelry.

39. Metti- Type of Silver Jewelry.

40. Mantra- prayer

41. Gayathri Mantra- Mantra that you say to Lord Surya or the Sun God.

42. Tabla- Instrument like drums.

43. Thalas- Beats

44. Gamakas- Glides of notes in songs.

45. Carnatic Music- south Indian Classical Music.

46. Hindustani Music- North Indian Classical Music.

47. Kaikeya- Country where Kaikeyi is from.

48. Manthara- Kaikeyi's companion who poisoned Kaikeyi's mind into sending Rama to the forest.

49. Dharma- Good Conduct.

50. Gandharva- Celestial being.

51. Abhivaadaye- Salutations.

52. Namaskaram- Falling on someone's foot for respect.

53. Guha- Captain of hunters.

54. Ashram- Home of Sage.

55. Sage Bharadwaja- Sage who told Rama to go to Chitrakuta.

56. Viradha- Son of Jaya who was killed by Rama.

57. Shurpanaka- Ravana's sister whose nose was cut off by Lakshmana.

58. Khara- Ravana's brother.

59. Dushana- Ravana's brother.

60. Jatayu- Dasharatha's friend who died trying to save Seetha when Ravana kidnapped her.

61. Mandodari- Ravana's wife.

62. Pushpak Aircraft- Ravana's aircraft.

63. Kabandha- Man cursed by a rishi and Lord Indra.

64. Vali- Brother of Sugriva who was killed by Rama.

65. Sugriva- King of Kishkindha.

66. Kishkindha- Kingdom where Sugriva was the king.

67. Shabari- Woman who had high devotion to Rama.

68. Hanuman- Minister of Sugriva and Devotee of Rama. Son of Anjana and Lord Vayu (the God of Wind).

69. Tara- Vali's wife.

70. Angada- Vali's son.

71. Sampati- Jatayu's brother who told Angada's army that Seetha was in Lanka.

72. Vibheeshana- Rakshasa who supported Rama and told Rama how to kill Ravana.

73. Akshay Kumar- Son of Ravana killed by Hanuman.

74. Indrajit- Son of Ravana killed by Lakshmana.

75. Sushena- Physician who told Hanuman to get the Sanjeevani and Vishalyani herbs.

76. Dharmayuddha- Rakshasa killed by Hanuman.

77. Varadaraja- Rakshasa killed by Angada.

78. Prahastha- Rakshasa killed by Neela.

79. Ankalampana- Rakshasa killed by Hanuman.

80. Sriman- Rakshasa killed by Lakshmana.

81. Kumbhakarna- Ravana's son killed by Sugriva.

82. Vaikuntha- heaven

83. Lord Shiva- Lord of Power. Nandi is his vehicle. Has three eyes.

84. Nandi- See Lord Shiva

85. Brahmin- In India, people followed a caste system.

A. Brahmin (most knowledgeable)

B. Kshatriya (warriors)

C. Vaishyas

D. Sudras (untouchables)

ABOUT THE AUTHOR

Girish Swaminath is a twelve-year-old boy born on January 23, 1992, in Santa Clara, California. He started to read and write at an early age. He has a big passion for writing. Girish wants to achieve three goals in life: to receive a good education, to become a doctor, and to translate epics for children. He is inspired by his intelligent older brother and his parents and is very thankful to them.

Printed in the United States
24321LVS00005B/121-255

9 781418 403812